THE WHOLE FIRST SECOND TEAM WISHES
TO EXTEND DEEP THANKS TO STUDIO GHIBLI
FOR THE CARE AND HELP AT EVERY STEP.

AND SPECIAL THANKS TO SYLVAIN COISSARD
FOR MAKING THIS PROJECT POSSIBLE.

:01 First Second

Published by First Second • First Second is an imprint of Roaring Brook Press, a division of Holtzbrinck Publishing Holdings Limited Partnership
120 Broadway, New York, NY 10271 • firstsecondbooks.com

 • First published in Japan by Tokuma Shoten Co., Ltd. Contract arranged through Sylvain Coissard Agency, France. • Library of Congress Cataloging-in-Publication Data is available.

Our books may be purchased in bulk for promotional, educational, or business use. Please contact your local bookseller or the Macmillan Corporate and Premium Sales Department at (800) 221-7945 ext. 5442 or by email at MacmillanSpecialMarkets@macmillan.com.

First American edition, 2022 • Translated by Alex Dudok de Wit • American edition edited by Mark Siegel and Kiara Valdez • Cover design by Kirk Benshoff • Interior book design by Kirk Benshoff, Sunny Lee, and Angela Boyle

Printed in Singapore

ISBN 978-1-250-84652-5 (hardcover)
10 9 8 7 6 5 4 3 2 1

Don't miss your next favorite book from First Second!
For the latest updates go to firstsecondnewsletter.com and sign up for our enewsletter.

The story line and general ambience of *Shuna's Journey* are also reflected in Miyazaki's *Princess Mononoke*, another project whose roots lie in his period of extraordinary creative ferment in the early 1980s. Ashitaka, the prince of an isolated village, is cursed by a demon god. He sets out west to find a cure and enters a world shaken by ecological calamity. Along the way, he sits by a campfire with an old man, who orients him toward a land of spirits inhospitable to humans; Shuna has the same experience. A version of Yakul, Ashitaka's elk-like steed, features in *Shuna's Journey*—although here "yakul" is the name of the species not an individual. Sharp-eyed readers will also spot early incarnations of the creatures sometimes referred to as minonohashi, which appear in both *Princess Mononoke* and *Castle in the Sky* (1986).

Revisiting *Shuna's Journey* almost four decades after its publication, we see the seeds of characters, motifs, and themes that will flourish in Miyazaki's later works. Historical significance aside, we read the book because it tells its story beautifully. I have compared it to *Nausicaä*, but in important ways, the two works are opposites. Where *Nausicaä* is epic, densely drawn and plotted, and laden with dialogue, *Shuna's Journey* is terse, spare, and lucent. It tackles some of the most adult subjects in the artist's oeuvre, but its language is as simple as a fable. At the same time, far more than the straightforward tale that inspired it, the book pulses with the kind of rich ambiguity that Miyazaki's fans know well. I hope it is as enjoyable to read as it was to translate.

ALEX DUDOK DE WIT

February 14, 2022 (Mon.)

September 1981, and the manga started serialization in the February 1982 issue of *Animage*. Meanwhile, the artist was developing the world of *Shuna's Journey*. In November 1982, he quit his job at animation studio Telecom Animation Film and was promptly approached to publish something under the newly launched Animage Bunko imprint, which was overseen by the magazine's editors. Thus, *Shuna's Journey* took shape as a book. Miyazaki finished it in May 1983—several months behind schedule—as preproduction on the feature adaptation of *Nausicaä* was getting underway. So it is little surprise that *Nausicaä* (both manga and film) and *Shuna's Journey* share many motifs and concerns: desert landscapes, vast tomb-like structures, dwindling natural resources, the figure of a monarch defending a small, windswept kingdom. Some pages in *Shuna's Journey* are almost indistinguishable from concept art published in the book *Nausicaä of the Valley of the Wind: Watercolor Impressions*.

Shuna's Journey also anticipates specific elements in Ghibli films. It is credited as an inspiration for *Tales from Earthsea*, a 2006 adaptation of Le Guin's novels directed by Miyazaki's son Gorō. The film reworks several scenes from *Shuna's Journey*, such as the protagonist's encounter with a sinister stranded ship, as well as its broader narrative structure: A boy rescues a girl from slavery and is later saved by her from dark magic. That Gorō borrowed from *Shuna's Journey* makes a kind of sense, considering that the Earthsea novels were surely on Miyazaki's mind when he was creating his book. Shuna comes across as a composite of the haughty Ged in *A Wizard of Earthsea* (the first novel in the series) and the melancholic Arren in *The Farthest Shore* (the third), and the latter novel is haunted by the specter of widespread social upheaval and spiritual malaise, just as *Shuna's Journey* is. (Curiously, the final chapter of *Shuna's Journey* is very similar in plot and setting to the fourth Earthsea novel, *Tehanu*, which was published in 1990—*after* Miyazaki's book. Great minds...)

In this sense, he differs from most questing Miyazaki heroes: Nausicaä, Sophie, Chihiro in *Spirited Away* (2001), Ashitaka in *Princess Mononoke*, and Conan in *Future Boy Conan* (1978) are all facing some kind of acute threat, and in several cases, they are encouraged on their way by those nearest to them. By leaving, Shuna actually defies his father and the community's elders. Later, he will disregard a warning about the danger of visiting the god-folk, then again ignore a voice that tells him not to steal the golden grain. He is punished for his hubris—although, whether the punishment comes from outside or within him is ambiguous—and is saved only once he has shown humility by (re)learning to work the land. His instinct to help others never evolves into a higher ideal of pacificism, as we see in Nausicaä or Ashitaka. Brooding and solitary, decent and daring, Shuna is a fitting hero for this most somber of Miyazaki's stories.

Miyazaki began work on *Shuna's Journey* around 1980, according to Toshio Suzuki, then an editor at the influential animation magazine *Animage,* and later Ghibli's producer. Miyazaki's feature directorial debut, *Lupin the 3rd: The Castle of Cagliostro*, had failed to set the box office alight on its release in late 1979, and his animation career was in a quiet stretch. Thus began a period of extraordinary creative brainstorming, as he developed visual and narrative concepts for a number of aborted films (and, often, for no project in particular). One of these films was to be an adaptation of Richard Corben's underground comic *Rowlf,* in which a princess is rescued by her loyal canine companion; we are reminded of *The Prince Who Turned into a Dog.* Another was a take on Ursula K. Le Guin's Earthsea novels, which foundered when permission to adapt them was refused. The project would be revived decades later and entwined with *Shuna's Journey.*

From this jumble of ideas, the worlds of *Nausicaä* and *Shuna's Journey* coalesced in tandem. Miyazaki began drawing *Nausicaä* in sterile seeds are then passed back to the traffickers, and people feed on them instead of growing their own crops. The precise workings of this trade remain unclear, as do the circumstances by which it arose. Yet it seems to say things about the hazards of our modern globalized economy. The god-folk's society is somehow fueled by slaves from elsewhere, not unlike how wealthy nations rely on overseas sweatshops to fulfill their material wants. Meanwhile, people have abandoned their land—whether voluntarily or not—and come to rely on imported food. (There is a parallel here with today's Japan, as others have noted.) Our lingering impression, as with other works by Miyazaki, is of a people grown estranged from nature, a world knocked askew by greed.

The slave narrative sets up the author's second great invention: Thea. The woman who will save Shuna is first saved by him, after he encounters her in chains, ready to be sold. By introducing this character early in the story, Miyazaki lays the groundwork for an emotionally satisfying climax: Shuna's arrival in Thea's mountain village marks a reunion, not a mere meeting, and this occasions a remarkable role reversal. Unlike the dog in the folktale, Shuna at this stage is delirious, so Thea must use her initiative to heal him and grow the barley. She has more to do than Goman. Here we have a prototypical Miyazaki heroine: a smart and driven woman who uses her agency to redeem the folly of humankind. She is cousin to Sophie in *Howl's Moving Castle* (2004), San in *Princess Mononoke* (1997), and of course Nausicaä.

There is indeed a kind of folly to Shuna, whose psychology is richer than Acho's. He has noble motives insofar as he generally wants to help those around him. Yet he pursues his mission with a streak of pride and a stubbornness verging on obsession. Crucially, his journey is not prompted by a crisis. While his people live hard lives, they have what they need to survive. But regardless, he is led on by the seductive promise of the seeds—of peace and plenty—and perhaps by the opportunity to prove his worth as a future king.

Miyazaki modeled the narrative of *Shuna's Journey* on a legend prevalent in what is now the Ngawa Tibetan and Qiang Autonomous Prefecture in Sichuan, China. The tale mythologizes Tibet's first encounter with barley, its staple crop to this day. In the Japanese translation read by Miyazaki, titled *Inu ni natta ōji* (*The Prince Who Turned into a Dog*), the young Prince Acho steals golden seeds from the lair of the Serpent King in the hope of feeding his impoverished people. But he is caught by the king, who turns him into a dog. Acho flees east (with the seeds) and reaches a village where he finds Goman, a beautiful maiden who loves all living things. She forms a strong attachment to the dog. During a ceremony in which she is to choose a husband, she accidentally indicates that she will marry the animal; for this, she is ridiculed and ostracized. At this point, the dog speaks, telling Goman he will walk ahead, sowing seeds as he goes. She follows the trail of cereal back to Acho's homeland, where she finds him returned to human form. They marry and live happily in a land now rich with grain.

Shuna's Journey preserves the essential shape of this story. Prince Shuna sets out west to find the rumored golden seeds, passing through environments that resemble iconic locations of Central Asia: the Silk Road city of Khiva and the Buddhas of Bamiyan (since destroyed by the Taliban). He eventually reaches a land where mysterious "god-folk" cultivate the golden grain, and he steals some. He suffers for his act, losing his mind and memory, but he is nursed back to health by the young woman Thea, in a mountain village. They succeed in growing the cereal, but we do not see Shuna return home.

At the same time, Miyazaki builds on his template, adding elements that radically change the tone and subtext of the tale. Strikingly, Shuna's quest for the seeds is folded into a larger narrative about slavery. We learn that traffickers supply the god-folk with humans and appear to receive grain in return. The hulled,

NOTE FROM THE TRANSLATOR

Much has been said of Hayao Miyazaki's fondness for using European settings in his films: the Adriatic of *Porco Rosso* (1992), say, or the pseudo-Sweden of *Kiki's Delivery Service* (1989). Less often mentioned is that Miyazaki has sometimes turned his gaze nearer west, to the cultures and landscapes of Asia. The continent's influence is particularly clear in a trio of printed works Miyazaki created in the first half of his career. We see it in his early manga *Sabaku no tami* (*People of the Desert*, 1969–70), a tale of warring Silk Road tribes. We sense it in *Nausicaä of the Valley of the Wind* (1982–94), his magnum opus of manga, whose teeming world bears the stamp of Indian, Chinese, and Central Asian scenery and civilizations. But his debt to Asia is perhaps most explicit in *Shuna's Journey*, whose story, as Miyazaki writes in his afterword, grew out of a folktale from Tibet.

Shuna's Journey was published in Japan in June 1983, two years before the launch of Studio Ghibli, the animation studio that would make Miyazaki globally famous. The book is not exactly a manga, reliant as it is on captions over speech bubbles, on detailed watercolor spreads over small panels: It is closer to what the Japanese would call an *emonogatari*, or an illustrated story. Although it continues to sell well in Japan, elsewhere *Shuna's Journey* has been generally overlooked by fans and scholars. No doubt this is partly because, until now, the book had never been published in translation. But it is a shame, as this slender volume brims with ideas that echo across Miyazaki's films and manga. At the same time, it is unique in his career: He has never produced another standalone *emonogatari* book. Nor, I think, has he ever told a story as beguilingly strange as this one.

AFTERWORD

This story is based on the Tibetan folktale *The Prince Who Turned into a Dog* (Zhi Jia, Jianbing Sun; translated into Japanese by Hisako Kimishima in an edition published by Iwanami Shoten). In the tale, the prince of a certain country is concerned that his people live in poverty, with no cereals to grow. At the end of a journey full of hardship, he steals grains from the Serpent King and, as a result, is magically turned into a dog. He is saved by the love of a young woman and eventually brings the cereal back to his country.

Today, barley is a staple in Tibet, but the crop apparently originated in West Asia and spread globally from there. So the narrative of the prince journeying west corresponds with history. But this folktale should not be viewed as a portrayal of actual events so much as an sublime story that arose from the Tibetan people's gratitude toward their crops.

After first reading the tale more than a decade ago, I long dreamed of adapting it in animation, but a project as unglamorous as this would not go far in Japan's current climate. I was giving up on the idea, thinking that if an animated version were ever to be made, it should be in China—but now, with the encouragement of the people at Tokuma Shoten, I have come up with a kind of visual adaptation of my own.

HAYAO MIYAZAKI
May 10, 1983 (Tue.)

SHUNA'S JOURNEY IS NOT YET OVER. THE ROAD TO THE VALLEY IS LONG, AND HIS TROUBLES ARE FAR FROM FINISHED—BUT THAT'S A STORY FOR ANOTHER TIME.

THE END

'5 1983

WHEN THE DAY CAME TO DEPART, THERE WERE ENOUGH GOLDEN SEEDS THAT SHUNA WAS ABLE TO LEAVE HALF TO THE VILLAGE.

THE VILLAGERS WERE SAD TO SEE THEM GO. EVEN THE OLD WOMAN, WHO STILL REGRETTED THAT SHE HADN'T FOUND A SON-IN-LAW, GAVE THEA HER LATE HUSBAND'S RIFLE.

BEFORE HE COULD RETURN TO HIS VALLEY, SHUNA SPENT ANOTHER YEAR IN THIS LAND. HE FOUGHT ALONGSIDE THE VILLAGERS AGAINST THE RAIDING MANHUNTERS, SOMETIMES EVEN BEATING THEM BACK TO THE DESERT. MEANWHILE, THE PLOT OF LAND GREW INTO A WHOLE FIELD OF GRAIN, AND THE SECOND HARVEST DWARFED THE FIRST.

THEY SAT SIDE BY SIDE, FILLED WITH A DEEP, PEACEFUL DELIGHT.
IT WAS OVER...
EVEN AT THAT VERY MOMENT, THE MOON WAS DASHING ACROSS THE SKY, AND MANHUNTERS WERE PROWLING THE LAND. BUT THE PAIR KNEW THEIR WORRIES WERE BEHIND THEM, AT LEAST FOR NOW.

SHUNA STOOD HOLDING A SHEAF OF GRAIN HE HAD REAPED, LOOKING LIKE SOMEONE WHO HAD JUST RETURNED FROM A LONG JOURNEY.
"SHUNA..."
MIYA

AUTUMN...

THE DAY CAME AT LAST.

THERE WAS A KNOCK ON THE DOOR.
THEA OPENED IT.

AS THE CROPS SLOWLY TOOK COLOR AND RIPENED, SO SHUNA CONTINUED TO RECOVER.

THEA BURST INTO FLOODS OF TEARS. SHE HAD NOT CRIED ONCE SINCE HER VILLAGE HAD BEEN BURNED DOWN. THE YOUNG WOMAN HUGGED SHUNA AND WEPT FIERCELY.
SHUNA HAD RECOVERED HIS SPEECH.

THE PAIR MANAGED TO KEEP THE PLOT SAFE. WHEN THE STORM HAD PASSED AND A BLUE SKY HAD RETURNED, THEA HEARD HER NAME BEING CALLED.
"THEA..."

AS SHE SPREAD A SHEET TO PROTECT THE PLOT OF LAND, THEA REASSURED SHUNA WITH WORDS OF ENCOURAGEMENT. LARGE HAILSTONES PUMMELED THEM AND FLATTENED THE GRASS. THE NIGHT TURNED PITCH-BLACK AS THE STORM ROARED AND RAGED...

THE BRIEF NORTHERN SUMMER CAME ROUND. AS THE SMALL PLOT OF LAND GREW THICK WITH GREEN, LIFE GRADUALLY RETURNED TO SHUNA'S FACE, TOO.
THEA RAN. ICE AND RAIN WERE SOON FALLING IN SLANTING SHEETS WHILE IT THUNDERED OVERHEAD.

ONE CLEAR DAY, AS THEA WAS OUT CUTTING THE GRASS OF A FAR-FLUNG MEADOW, A CHILL WIND WHIPPED PAST, AND DARK CLOUDS ROLLED IN FROM THE MOUNTAINS.
MIYA'83

THE WHOLE VILLAGE RESOUNDED WITH LAUGHTER.
THE PROUD YAKUL DEFTLY USED HIS HORNS TO THROW EACH RIDER OFF IN TURN.

WHEN THE LAST SUITOR HAD FAILED, THEA'S LITTLE SISTER STEPPED FORWARD, LEADING AN UNFAMILIAR YOUNG MAN BY THE HAND. HE WORE CLOTHES WOVEN FROM THE YAKUL'S FUR. THE VILLAGERS UNDERSTOOD AT ONCE: HERE WAS A MASTER WITH HIS TRUSTY STEED... SHUNA NIMBLY MOUNTED THE YAKUL, LEAPED OVER THE RING OF VILLAGERS, AND RAN OFF. THE OLD WOMAN WAS BITTERLY DISAPPOINTED, BUT THE VILLAGERS WENT HOME SATISFIED.

WHEN THE DAY CAME, THE WHOLE VILLAGE GATHERED TO WATCH THEA CHOOSE HER GROOM.

THE OLD WOMAN HAD DECKED THEA OUT IN THE FINERY THE WOMAN HAD WORN IN HER OWN YOUTH. THE SIGHT OF THEA CAUSED QUITE A STIR AMONG THE YOUNG MEN.
SHE SAID, "I WILL MARRY THE MAN WHO IS ABLE TO RIDE OUR YAKUL."

ONE DAY, AS THE MIDSUMMER FESTIVAL APPROACHED, THE OLD WOMAN CALLED THEA OVER: "YOU'VE COME OF AGE, AND I WANT A STRONG WORKER." SHE WAS TELLING THEA TO PICK A HUSBAND FROM AMONG THE YOUNG MEN OF THE VILLAGE. "IF YOU DON'T WANT TO, YOU CAN LEAVE." THEA SAID IT WAS TOO SOON, BUT HER WORDS WENT UNHEEDED. ON THE EVE OF THE FESTIVAL, THEA FINISHED SEWING SHUNA'S CLOTHES FROM HER WOVEN CLOTH.

SEEING THE GREEN SEEDLINGS, THEA'S LITTLE SISTER LET OUT A JOYOUS LAUGH. THE GIRL HADN'T LAUGHED ONCE SINCE THE MANHUNTERS HAD SET HER HOMELAND ABLAZE, BUT NOW SHE WAS TWIRLING ALL ABOUT.
FROM THAT MOMENT, A FAINT SMILE RETURNED TO SHUNA'S FACE, TOO.

IT WAS THE FIRE BURNING BY SHUNA'S HIDEOUT. HER SISTER WAS IN CHARGE OF COLLECTING A LITTLE WOOD EVERY DAY AND LIGHTING THE FIRE.
NO MATTER HOW EXHAUSTED SHE WAS, THE SIGHT OF THE SMALL LIGHT UP ON THE MOUNTAIN ALWAYS WARMED HER HEART.

ONE MORNING...
...SHUNA HAD CRAWLED OUT ON HIS OWN AND WAS STARING AT THE PLOT OF LAND. THE GOLDEN SEEDS HAD ALL SPROUTED AT ONCE.

SHUNA CLUTCHED HIS POUCH, RELUCTANT TO SOW THE SEEDS. SLOWLY AND PATIENTLY, THEA SHOWED HIM HOW TO DO IT. HAVING SOWN THE SEEDS, SHUNA WOULD DIG THEM BACK UP DURING THE NIGHT AND RETURN THEM TO HIS POUCH.

EVERY DAY, AS THE VILLAGE STILL SLEPT, SHE BROUGHT HIM FOOD AND WATER. THE OLD WOMAN KEPT GRUMBLING THAT SUPPLIES WERE DISAPPEARING QUICKLY, BUT THEA CONTINUED TO BRING SHUNA HIS FOOD, EVEN WHEN IT MEANT GIVING HIM SOME OF HER SHARE.

SPRING ARRIVED LATE. EARLY ONE MORNING, THEA TOOK SHUNA OUTSIDE.
SHE PLOWED A PATCH OF WASTELAND FAR FROM THE VILLAGE AND CREATED A SMALL PLOT. THEN SHE DUG ROCKS UP AND PILED THEM TO MAKE A HIDEOUT FOR SHUNA.

WINTER CAME. HUDDLED IN HIS CORNER, SHUNA SLEPT THROUGH THE LONG, DARK SEASON, WAKING ONLY TO EAT. THEA DIDN'T MENTION HIM TO THE OLD WOMAN OR ANY OF THE VILLAGERS.

THEA PEEKED INSIDE THE POUCH THAT SHUNA CARRIED PROTECTIVELY AROUND HIS NECK.

THE SIGHT BROUGHT A LUMP TO HER THROAT AND TEARS TO HER EYES.
THE GOLDEN GRAIN...

THEA THREADED A NEEDLE AND BEGAN TO SEW CLOTHES FOR SHUNA OUT OF CLOTH SHE HAD LYING AROUND... SHE COULDN'T BEGIN TO GUESS WHAT HAD HAPPENED TO HIM.
SHE JUST KNEW ONE THING: IT WAS HER TURN TO HELP.

THEA LED SHUNA TO THE STOREROOM WHERE SHE LIVED WITH HER SISTER. SHUNA HAD LOST EVERYTHING: HIS MEMORY, HIS SPEECH, HIS NAME, EVEN HIS FEELINGS. AFRAID OF THE FIRE, HE JUST COWERED WHERE IT WAS DARK AND DEVOURED HIS FOOD.

SHE CALLED SHUNA'S NAME. HE SLOWLY TURNED AROUND. HIS EYES WERE VACANT.
THEA MOUNTED THE YAKUL, NOT EVEN PAUSING TO SADDLE HIM, AND TOOK THE ROAD THAT WENT SOUTH. WHEN SHE CAME TO THE EDGE OF THE VILLAGE, SHE SAW A GHOSTLY FIGURE WALKING AHEAD, DOWN THE UNPOPULATED ROAD THAT LED TO THE GULLY.

THE VILLAGERS WERE ROUGH IN THEIR WAYS, YET THEY HAD WELCOMED THE SISTERS WARMLY, FOR THEY HATED THE SLAVE TRADERS AND LOVED THOSE WHO WORKED HARD LIKE THEY DID.

THAT NIGHT, SHE FELT PARTICULARLY UNSETTLED. THE YAKUL TOO WAS RESTLESS; HIS NOSE KEPT TWITCHING EAGERLY.
SUDDENLY, THEA THOUGHT SHE COULD HEAR SHUNA'S VOICE CALLING FOR HELP.

THE PAIR WERE ALWAYS HUNGRY—BUT THEN SO WAS ALMOST EVERYONE IN THIS VILLAGE.

WHAT HAD BECOME OF SHUNA? THEA WAS SMART, SO SHE KNEW THERE WAS NOTHING TO DO BUT PATIENTLY WAIT. BUT WHEN SHE WORRIED ABOUT SHUNA, HER HEART FELT AS THOUGH IT MIGHT BREAK.
THEA WAS A STRONG YOUNG WOMAN: SHE COMPLAINED TO NO ONE. BUT WHEN THE BUSY DAY WAS DONE, SHE WOULD BE SEIZED BY AN OVERWHELMING YEARNING.

THE WOMAN WAS STINGY AND MEAN, BUT SHE WASN'T A BAD PERSON.
THEA KNEW WELL THAT UNHAPPY OLD PEOPLE HAVE A TENDENCY TO NAG.
MIYA

THEY WERE STAYING WITH AN OLD WOMAN WHO LIVED ALONE, WITH NOBODY ELSE LEFT TO SUPPORT HER. THERE WERE ALWAYS THINGS TO BE DONE, BUT THE SISTERS WORKED HARD, AND THE YAKUL WAS A STRONG HELPER.

NEARLY A YEAR HAD PASSED
SINCE THEA AND HER LITTLE
SISTER HAD FLED TO THIS POOR
VILLAGE IN THE NORTH.

THEA

HE RAN IN A FRENZY, EMERGING FROM THE FOREST TO FIND THE SEA RAGING. REELING FROM THE PAIN, HE LEAPED INTO THE DARK WATERS.

GRITTING HIS TEETH, CLUTCHING THE GRAIN, SHUNA RAN.
AT ONCE, HIS BODY CONVULSED WITH A TERRIBLE SHOCK, AND A SHARP PAIN PIERCED HIS HEART.

THE MOMENT SHUNA'S HAND TOUCHED THE EAR, THE GIANTS BEGAN TO WRITHE ABOUT AND CRY, "OOOOHHH... OOOOHHH," AS THOUGH WEEPING OR PRAYING. AT THE SAME TIME, SHUNA HEARD A VOICE RESOUND FROM DEEP WITHIN HIM: "STOP. STOP." HE PLUCKED SOME EARS ANYWAY.

THE EARS OF GRAIN HAD ALREADY STARTED TAKING ON COLOR.
THIS WAS NO PLACE TO LINGER: TIME FLOWED DIFFERENTLY HERE.
SHUNA CROSSED THE CANAL.

SHUNA LOOKED AT HIS RIFLE BESIDE HIM, AND HIS BREATH CAUGHT.

IN THE SPACE OF JUST HALF A DAY, IT HAD TURNED RUSTY. HIS SWORD AND CLOTHES TOO HAD BECOME WORN.

BY MIDDAY,
EARS OF GRAIN
WERE APPEARING.

THE GIANTS WORKED TIRELESSLY, SCOOPING WATER UP AND SPRINKLING IT ON THE FIELDS. AS THE SUN ROSE, THE FIRST SEEDLINGS APPEARED.

ONCE THE VAST MASS HAD SWALLOWED ALL THE PEOPLE UP, IT BEGAN TO ROCK SLOWLY. SOME TIME PASSED. EVENTUALLY, WHEN THE MOON'S LIGHT HAD DIMMED AND CALM HAD RETURNED, PHOSPHORESCENT WATER CAME FLOWING OUT FROM THOSE HOLES AND BEGAN TO FILL THE CANALS AROUND THE FIELDS. THAT'S WHEN SHUNA SAW THEM: COUNTLESS FIGURES RISING UP FROM THE WATER. THEY WERE GREEN GIANTS, NEWLY BORN.

SHUNA COULDN'T TELL WHETHER THE PEOPLE, AFTER BEING SWALLOWED, HAD BEEN REBORN AS GIANTS OR TURNED INTO THE WATER THAT IRRIGATED THE LAND. THE GIANTS SPREAD OUT ACROSS THE FIELDS, SWAYING SLIGHTLY, AND STARTED SCATTERING THE GOLDEN SEEDS FROM THEIR MOUTHS.

THINGS STARTED POURING OUT FROM WHERE THE MOON'S MOUTH WAS. HUMANS!

WHAT THE OLD MAN HAD SAID WAS TRUE. THESE WERE NONE OTHER THAN THE PEOPLE THE GOD-FOLK HAD COLLECTED FROM THE SLAVE TRADERS.

IN THE MIDDLE OF THE NIGHT, THE MOON RETURNED. IT CAME TO A HALT RIGHT ABOVE THE STRUCTURE.

INSIDE, A SWEET SCENT EMANATED FROM THE PITCH-BLACK GLOOM. SHUNA TOOK ONE STEP INTO THE HOLE. AS SOON AS HE DID SO, ALL HIS HAIR STOOD ON END, AND HE WAS SEIZED WITH DREAD. HE RAN BACK TO THE FOREST, ALMOST TUMBLING OVER AS HE WENT.

THAT WASN'T A BUILDING. IT WAS ALIVE. IT WAS DEFINITELY BREATHING...

SHUNA COULDN'T SEE ANYTHING THAT LOOKED LIKE AN ENTRANCE— ONLY HOLES AROUND THE BASE, OUT OF WHICH RAN THE CANALS.

THE BUILDING WAS MADE OF NEITHER STONE NOR METAL; IT WAS WARM AND STRANGELY ELASTIC TO THE TOUCH.
MIYA

AS HE WALKED ON, SHUNA PASSED MORE AND MORE GIANTS. LIKE PEOPLE GOING OFF TO REST TOGETHER, THEY FADED INTO THE DEPTHS OF THE FOREST, QUIVERING FAINTLY AS THEY WENT.
SUDDENLY, THE TREES THINNED OUT.
SOME KIND OF MYSTERIOUS BUILDING TOWERED OVER OPEN FARMLAND. THE WELL-PLOWED FIELDS WERE CRISSCROSSED WITH WHAT LOOKED LIKE CANALS.

STARTING BACK DOWN THE PATH THE GIANT HAD TAKEN, SHUNA IMMEDIATELY RAN INTO ANOTHER ONE. THEY WERE FACE-TO-FACE, YET THE GIANT SEEMED TO TAKE NO NOTICE OF SHUNA, AND WALKED PAST HIM WITH A SERENE EXPRESSION. IT WAS WOUNDED. "IT HAS GONE TO DIE," SHUNA WHISPERED WITH A SHUDDER.

SHUNA COULD HARDLY WATCH WHAT HAPPENED NEXT. A PACK OF SMALL ANIMALS COVERED THE GIANT AND BEGAN TO EAT IT.

WHEN IT REACHED A CLEARING IN THE FOREST, THE GIANT HALTED.

THEN IT SLOWLY TOPPLED OVER.

WAS IT ONE OF THE GOD-FOLK? THE OLD MAN'S WORDS FLITTED THROUGH SHUNA'S MIND: THEY DON'T LIKE IT WHEN HUMANS COME.
SOMEONE'S THERE!

IT WAS A GREEN GIANT. IT WALKED SILENTLY AND A LITTLE UNSTEADILY, A THRONG OF BEASTS AND INSECTS FOLLOWING BEHIND.

NOTHING HERE WAS DANGEROUS, NOTHING IN DANGER. SHUNA WAS FILLED WITH A SENSE OF PROFOUND CALM.

AH, BUT WHAT A
LUSH, PEACEFUL
WORLD THIS WAS!

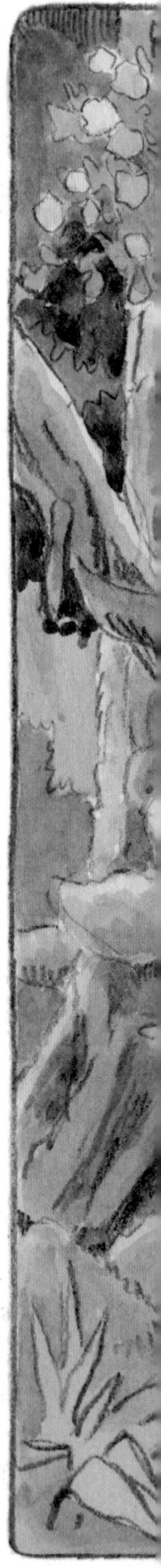

THE ISLAND WAS COVERED BY DENSE WOODLAND THAT NO HUMAN FEET HAD EVER DISTURBED. SHUNA PUSHED ON, PENETRATING EVER DEEPER INTO THE FOREST.

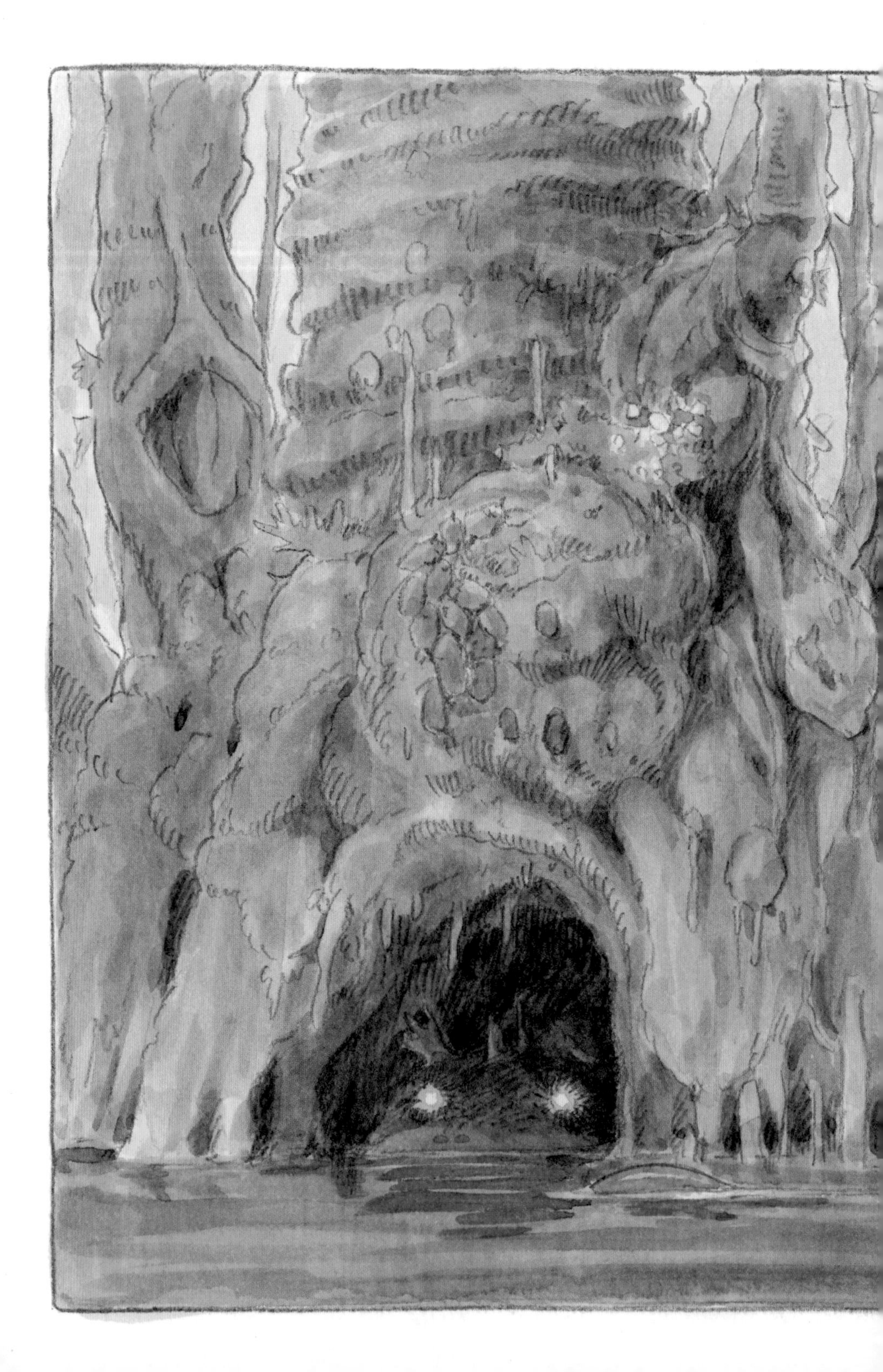

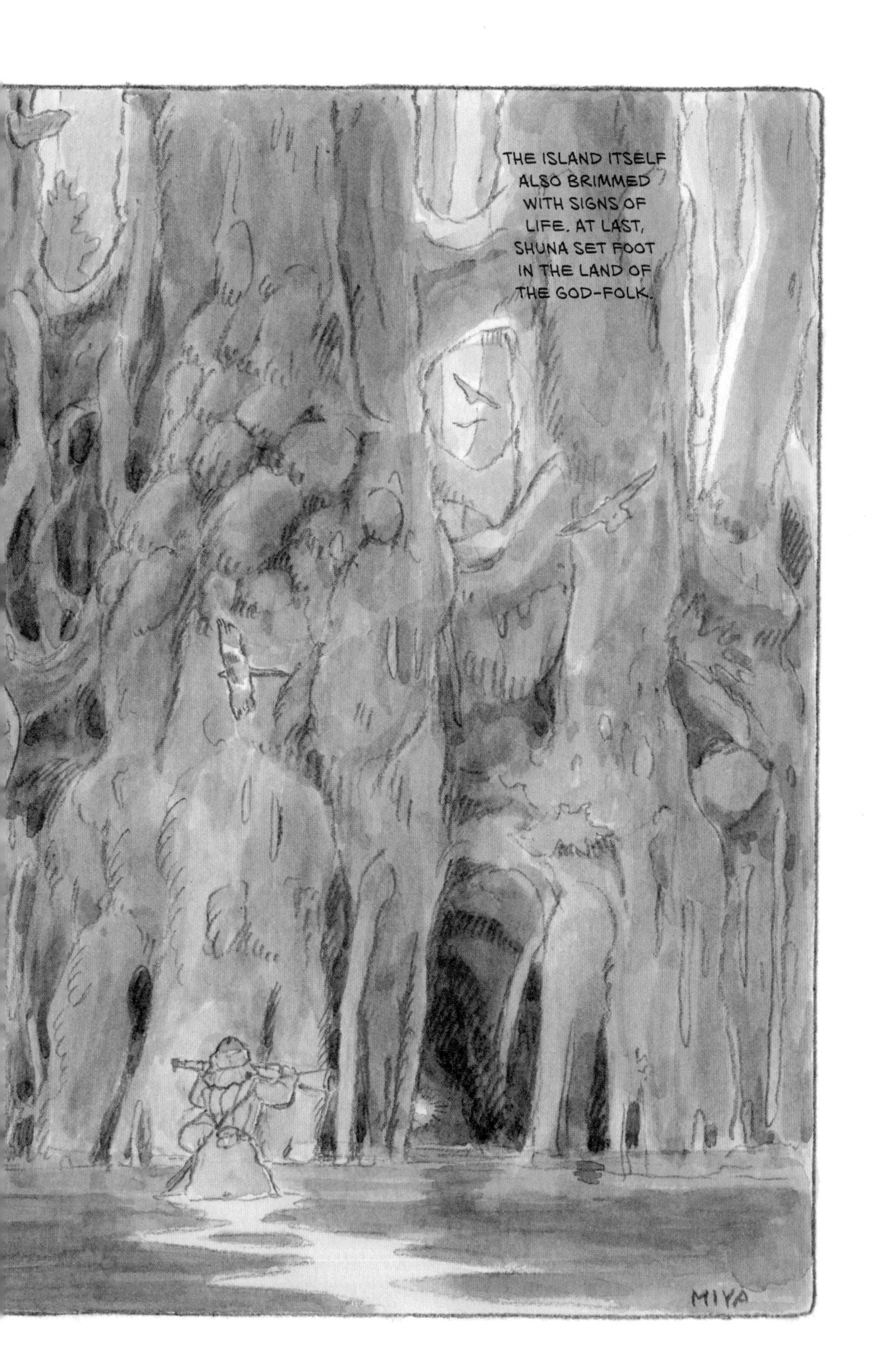
THE ISLAND ITSELF
ALSO BRIMMED
WITH SIGNS OF
LIFE. AT LAST,
SHUNA SET FOOT
IN THE LAND OF
THE GOD-FOLK.
MIYA

AS HE WALKED ACROSS
THE SHALLOWS TOWARD
THE ISLAND, THE TIDE
BEGAN TO EBB. THE SEA
WAS FULL OF CREATURES.
SPECIES THOUGHT TO HAVE
DIED OUT LONG AGO LIVED
ON IN THESE WATERS.

SHUNA AWOKE TO FIND THAT HE WAS LYING IN WARM, CLEAR WATER. AT SOME POINT, THE TIDE HAD COME IN.

IT WAS A DIFFERENT WORLD: ALL WAS CALM AND BRIGHT. HE COULD NOW SEE SANDBARS THAT WAVES HAD HIDDEN THE DAY BEFORE.

THE LAND OF THE GOD-FOLK LAY ON THE FAR SIDE OF A STORMY SEA.
CROUCHING DOWN ON THE SPOT, SHUNA FELT THE STRENGTH LEAVE HIS BODY. HE SANK INTO A SLEEP AS DEEP AS THE SEA.

EXHAUSTED AND
UNSURE WHAT
TO DO, SHUNA
STAGGERED
INTO THE WATER
AND WASHED HIS
FACE, HANDS,
AND FEET. THE
WATER WAS
PAINFULLY COLD.

WHAT NOW?

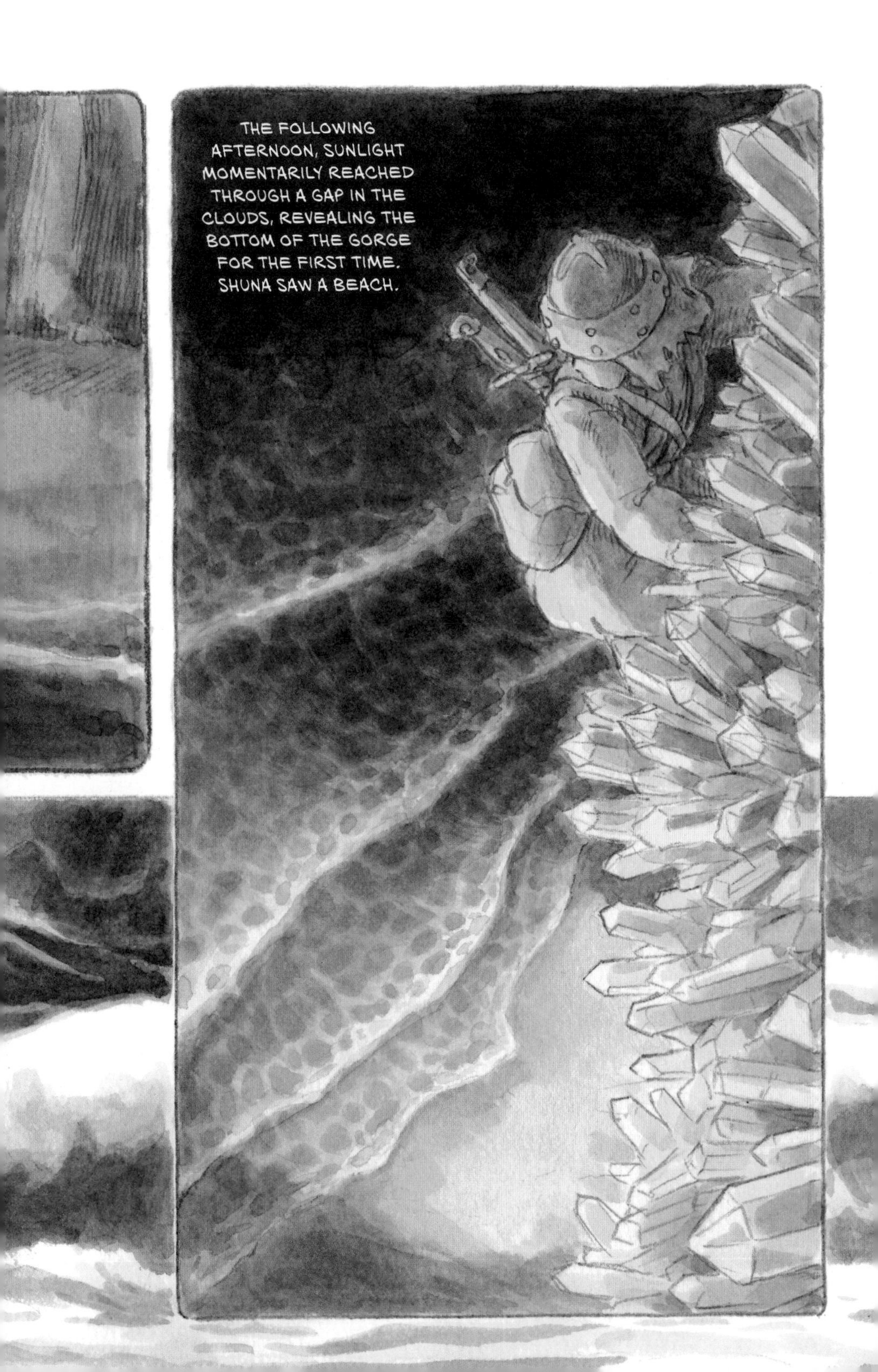
THE FOLLOWING AFTERNOON, SUNLIGHT MOMENTARILY REACHED THROUGH A GAP IN THE CLOUDS, REVEALING THE BOTTOM OF THE GORGE FOR THE FIRST TIME. SHUNA SAW A BEACH.

SHUNA PENETRATED THE CLOUDS, ENTERING A WORLD OF DARKNESS BARELY TOUCHED BY THE SUN. VISIBILITY PLUMMETED; THE GODS DISAPPEARED FROM VIEW. SHUNA MADE HIS WAY DOWN ALONG THE SKELETONS OF PRIMEVAL DRAGONS THAT PROTRUDED FROM THE ROCK FACE. HE SPENT HIS FIRST NIGHT PERCHED ON A BONE.

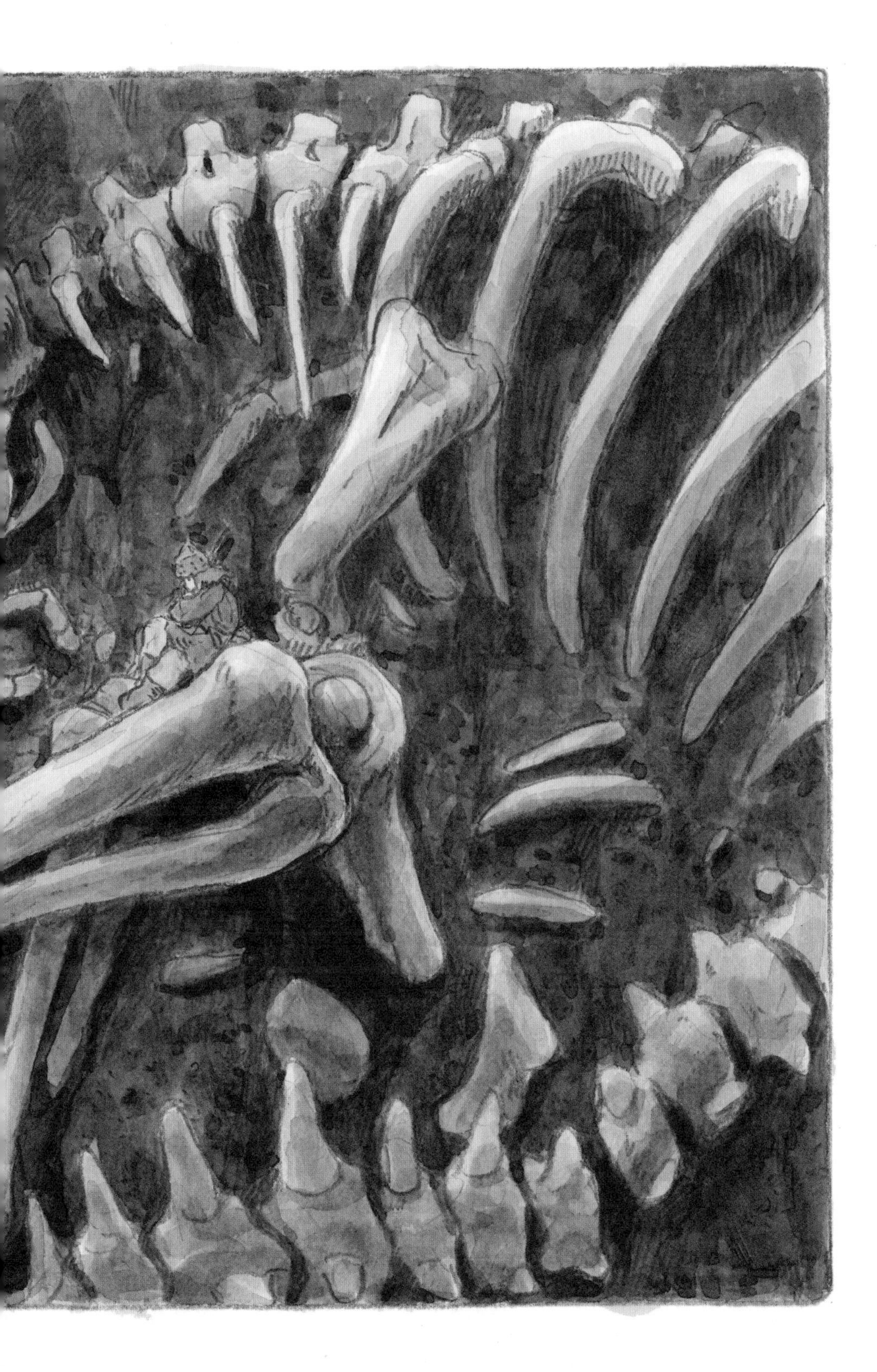

HE DISCOVERED THAT COUNTLESS
ANCIENT GODS, INVISIBLE FROM THE TOP,
HAD BEEN CARVED INTO THE CLIFF.
THERE THEY HAD BEEN ABANDONED, THEIR
NAMES LONG SINCE FORGOTTEN. AS SHUNA
DESCENDED, HE COULD JUST ABOUT GRIP
THE HANDHOLDS THEY PROVIDED.

THE LAND
OF THE
GOD-FOLK
NIGHT TURNED TO DAY, BUT THE AIR WAS
THICK WITH DUST, CONCEALING THE FAR
SHORE, AND DENSE CLOUDS BLANKETED
THE VALLEY FLOOR. STEELING HIMSELF,
SHUNA STARTED CLIMBING DOWN THE
VERTICAL CLIFF FACE.

IT FADED INTO THE DISTANCE, TRAILING A LONG TAIL OF LIGHT. FOR AN INSTANT, THE FAR SHORE WAS SILHOUETTED AMID THE DARKNESS.
THAT WAS THE LAND OF THE GOD-FOLK, WHERE THE OLD MAN HAD SAID THE MOON IS BORN AND RETURNS TO DIE. THERE, SURELY, HE WOULD FIND THE GOLDEN SEEDS.

THAT WAS WHEN IT HAPPENED: SHUNA WAS BATHED IN A BLUE-WHITE LIGHT LIKE THE GLOW OF A HUNDRED MOONS.

IT WAS A GIANT, SHINING FACE—A MOON STREAKING ACROSS THE SKY WITH TERRIFIC SPEED.

AS SOON AS THE LAST PURSUER WAS AMONG THE MOUNDS, SHUNA ROSE.

ONE AFTER ANOTHER, HIS BULLETS FOUND THE CAREFULLY LAID SHELLS, SETTING THEM OFF WITH A BOOM AND A FLASH. THE BEASTS PANICKED AND BOLTED TOWARD THE CLIFF.

WHEN SHE REALIZED THE PURPOSE OF HIS JOURNEY, THE GIRL CAST DOWN HER EYES. AFTER A WHILE, SHE LOOKED UP AND SAID: "IF YOU MAKE IT BACK FROM THE LAND OF THE GOD-FOLK, PLEASE HEAD NORTH AND KEEP GOING. WE'LL BE WAITING FOR YOU THERE, HOWEVER LONG IT TAKES." THE GIRL SAID HER NAME WAS THEA. SHUNA DIVIDED THE FOOD AND WATER IN HALF. WHEN THE TIME CAME TO LEAVE, THEA AND HER LITTLE SISTER WAVED ONCE, THEN WITHOUT LOOKING BACK AGAIN, HURRIED NORTHWARD AND OUT OF SIGHT.

REMEMBERING HOW HE WOULD TRAP GOATS WHEN OUT HUNTING IN THE VALLEY, SHUNA ENCLOSED A SPACE AROUND THE CLIFF EDGE BY GATHERING STONES INTO LITTLE MOUNDS AND LAYING SHELLS INSIDE.

THEN HE DUG A HOLE IN THE SAND, HID HIMSELF, AND WAITED IN SILENCE.

"THE YAKUL CAN KEEP RUNNING IF IT'S JUST THE TWO OF YOU. I'LL STAY HERE AND STOP THEM." THE OLDER GIRL SAID THEY TOO WOULD STAY, BUT SHUNA REPLIED, "ONCE I'M DONE WITH THE PURSUERS, I WILL GO ON TO THE LAND OF THE GOD-FOLK."

TWO NIGHTS LATER, THE GROUND BEFORE THEM ABRUPTLY DISAPPEARED. THEY HAD REACHED THE WORLD'S EDGE—THE PLACE OF WHICH THE OLD MAN HAD SPOKEN.
THEY SLEPT WHILE RUNNING. THEY RAN WHILE EATING.

THE PURSUERS WERE WAITING FOR THE YAKUL TO TIRE. AS THE ANIMAL WOVE BETWEEN THE SHADOWS ON THE HORIZON, THEY STEADILY FOLLOWED HIS TRACKS, AND SHUNA SENSED THEIR PRESENCE BEHIND HIM AT ALL TIMES.

CARRYING THE TRIO, THE YAKUL RACED WESTWARD AT LIGHTNING SPEED, AND THE PURSUERS SWIFTLY DROPPED OUT OF SIGHT. BUT SHUNA SAW THAT THEY WERE SKILLED AT GIVING CHASE: THEY WERE MAKING SURE NOT TO RUN TOO FAST.

1983.

"THIS FREEDOM WASN'T BOUGHT. I SWORE BY MY SWORD THAT I WOULD FIGHT FOR YOUR HONOR. YOU ARE FREE."

NO SOONER HAD HE SPOKEN THAN PURSUERS FROM THE TOWN APPEARED ON THE HORIZON. "LET'S GO!" SAID SHUNA, LIFTING THE GIRLS ONTO THE SADDLE.

SHUNA FOUND THE KEYS AND OPENED THE IRON DOOR. "COME OUT IF YOU DESIRE FREEDOM, EVEN IF IT MEANS SPENDING YOUR LIFE ON THE RUN."

ONLY THE TWO SISTERS EMERGED. THE OTHERS STAYED PUT, FEARING REPRISALS.

SPOTTING THE SLAVE TRADERS' VEHICLE, SHUNA GOT IN FRONT OF IT AND UNLEASHED A BURST OF FIRE AT POINT-BLANK RANGE. THE ATTACK CAUGHT THEM COMPLETELY OFF GUARD. SHUNA KEPT FIRING WITH WICKED COMPOSURE, AS HE WOULD WHEN HUNTING SNOW LEOPARDS. BY THE TIME HE HAD RUN A RING AROUND THE VEHICLE, HE HAD SHOT THEM ALL DOWN.

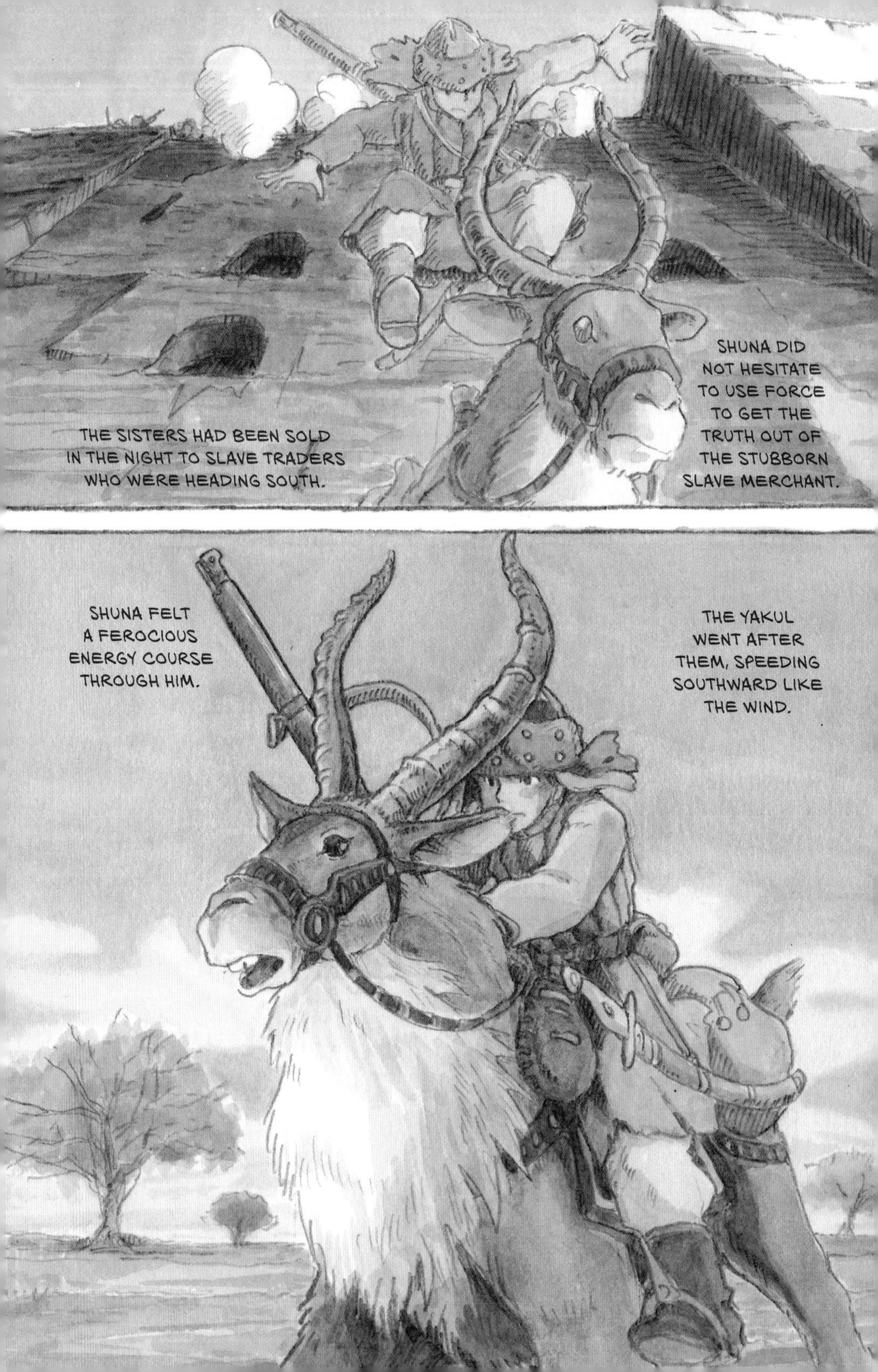
THE SISTERS HAD BEEN SOLD
IN THE NIGHT TO SLAVE TRADERS
WHO WERE HEADING SOUTH.
SHUNA DID
NOT HESITATE
TO USE FORCE
TO GET THE
TRUTH OUT OF
THE STUBBORN
SLAVE MERCHANT.
SHUNA FELT
A FEROCIOUS
ENERGY COURSE
THROUGH HIM.
THE YAKUL
WENT AFTER
THEM, SPEEDING
SOUTHWARD LIKE
THE WIND.

SHUNA RETURNED TO THE TOWN TO FIND THE PLACE STILL SOUND ASLEEP, ITS GATES FIRMLY SHUT. HE SCALED THE RAMPART AND WENT BACK TO THE ALLEY, BUT THE SISTERS HAD GONE, LEAVING ONLY THE SHACKLES CHAINED TO THE WALL.

"WHETHER YOU GO IS UP TO YOU."
WITH THAT, THE OLD MAN WENT TO SLEEP.
JUST BEFORE DAWN, SHUNA OPENED HIS EYES TO FIND THE MAN GONE. SHUNA SET OFF—FIRST, TOWARD THE EAST...

"KEEP HEADING WEST. YOU'LL KNOW YOU'VE REACHED THE WORLD'S END WHEN YOU COME TO A PRECIPICE. BEYOND IS THE LAND OF THE GOD-FOLK, WHERE THE MOON IS BORN AND RETURNS TO DIE."

"THE GOD-FOLK...?"

"PEOPLE USED TO POSSESS THE GOLDEN GRAIN. THEY'D HARVEST THE CROP AND PLANT THE SEEDS THEMSELVES, AND THAT'S WHAT THEY LIVED ON. BUT NOW ONLY THE GOD-FOLK HAVE THE GRAIN. PEOPLE STARTED SELLING HUMANS TO THE GOD-FOLK IN RETURN FOR DEAD SEEDS.

"THE GOD-FOLK DON'T LIKE IT WHEN PEOPLE COME NEAR. NO ONE HAS EVER RETURNED FROM THAT LAND."

IN THAT CASE, WHY DON'T YOU HEAD HOME AT ONCE? BACK TO THE COZY, SHIELDED LIFE OF A PRINCE...

BEST NOT TO GO LOOKING FOR ANY GOLDEN SEEDS.
OUCH!

"WOULD YOU HAPPEN TO KNOW WHERE I CAN FIND THE SEEDS?"
"I MIGHT KNOW SOMETHING ABOUT IT."
"PLEASE TELL ME HOW TO GET THERE."
"HEE HEE... FIRST, LET ME HAVE ANOTHER OF THOSE BREAD ROLLS..."

GOOD LUCK COMES TO THOSE WHO SHOW KINDNESS TO THE ELDERLY! RIGHT, HOW 'BOUT SOME OF THAT BREAD? HEE HEE...

"AH, THE SLAVE MARKET..."
"I THOUGHT I COULD HELP THE PEOPLE OF MY VALLEY BY SEARCHING FOR THE GOLDEN SEEDS. BUT I COULDN'T EVEN SAVE ONE GIRL RIGHT THERE IN FRONT OF ME..."
"HEE HEE... AND NOW YOU'VE LOST FAITH IN YOUR JOURNEY?"

OOH, A FIRE!
GOT ROOM FOR A
POOR OLD MAN?
I'M FROZEN
STIFF.

TEARS RUSHED TO HIS EYES. HE WIPED THEM AWAY, BUT STILL, THEY KEPT STREAMING OUT.
MIYA

IF YOU DON'T WANT TO DIE, KEEP QUIET.
SHUNA TRIED TO INTERVENE BUT FOUND HIMSELF SURROUNDED BY GUARDS.
GET OUT OF MY SIGHT, BEGGAR. UNLESS YOU WANT TO HEAR HER SHRIEK SOME MORE?

THERE WAS NOTHING TO DO BUT LEAVE...

"DON'T!" THE OLDER GIRL STOOD UP SUDDENLY.

IF YOU GET RID OF YOUR WEAPON, THEY'LL KIDNAP YOU TOO BEFORE YOU KNOW IT.
ALSO, WE'RE NOT ROYALTY OR ANYTHING. BUT WE DON'T WANT TO BE BOUGHT—NOT EVEN BY YOU.

"SHUT IT!" "I'LL SHOW YOU WHO'S BOSS."

THESE SISTERS HAVE ROYAL BLOOD IN 'EM.

THEY'D MAKE FINE WIVES. FINE SERVANTS, TOO. I'LL GIVE YOU A SPECIAL PRICE.

IF IT MEANT HE COULD FREE THE GIRLS...

SHUNA HESITATED.

IF HE GAVE THE YAKUL AWAY, THAT WOULD BE THE END OF HIS JOURNEY—AND HIS JEWEL WAS GONE.

D'YOU LIKE THESE TWO, MR. TRAVELER, SIR? YOU HAVE A GOOD EYE.

EVEN CHILDREN THIS YOUNG...

EAT.

THE MEN WERE TIGHT-LIPPED. WHEREVER SHUNA WENT, HE WAS MET WITH A WALL OF HOSTILE SILENCE.

HE WAS TIRED...
1983

SHUNA FROZE BEFORE ONE OF THE HEAPS. THERE WERE THE SEEDS HE HAD BEEN SEARCHING FOR. BUT THEY HAD ALL BEEN THRESHED: THEY WERE DEAD. SHUNA ASKED THE MERCHANT WHETHER HE HAD ANY LIVING ONES.

"NO ONE TENDS THE FIELDS ANYMORE. NOWADAYS, YOU CAN GET AS MUCH GRAIN AS YOU NEED FROM ELSEWHERE."

"SO WHERE DO THEY GROW IT?"

"THE SLAVE TRADERS BRING IT TO EXCHANGE FOR PEOPLE. ASK THEM."

THE MERCHANT'S MANNER PROMPTLY CHANGED WHEN SHUNA SHOWED THE MAN THE JEWEL IN HIS SWORD'S HILT. THE STOREFRONT WAS LINED WITH HEAPS OF DIFFERENT GRAINS AND BEANS.

WHAT WAS GOING ON...? THE MAIN COMMODITY TRADED IN THIS TOWN WAS HUMAN BEINGS.

THE CLUSTERED TOWERS WERE STARTING TO CRUMBLE, BUT THE TOWN BUSTLED WITH LIFE. SHUNA HAD NEVER SEEN ANYTHING LIKE IT.

ON ALL FOUR SIDES,
THE WALLS WERE PIERCED
BY GREAT GATES, THROUGH
WHICH STREAMED
A CONSTANT TRAFFIC OF
PEOPLE AND VEHICLES.
IN THE
FORTRESS
TOWN

THE WAGON
WAS PACKED
WITH PEOPLE.
WHAT HAD
HAPPENED
HERE?

AS SHUNA PASSED COUNTLESS
MORE VEHICLES LIKE IT, THE
SPRAWL OF A TOWN APPEARED
ON THE BARREN PLAIN.

CONTINUING WESTWARD, SHUNA CAME ACROSS A LARGE WAGON PULLED BY BEASTS. HE ASKED WHERE THE ROAD LED, BUT THE MEN JUST LAUGHED AT HIS OLD-FASHIONED RIFLE AND IGNORED THE QUESTION.
A STRANGE SMELL EMANATED FROM THE ARMORED VEHICLE. WITH A SHOCK, SHUNA SAW WHAT WAS INSIDE.

WHERE ON EARTH HAD THE INHABITANTS GONE?

THE FIELDS HAD TURNED WILD AGAIN, THE CROPS NOW PRODUCING EVEN LESS THAN THE HIWABIE.
NO GOLDEN SEEDS HERE...

THE AIR THICKENED. BEFORE LONG, VILLAGE AFTER VILLAGE CAME INTO VIEW, ALL OF THEM ABANDONED.

WHEN THE SUPPLIES THEY HAD BROUGHT FROM THE VALLEY RAN OUT, SHUNA AND THE YAKUL WENT HUNGRY.
TIME GRADUALLY LOST ITS MEANING UNTIL SHUNA COULD NO LONGER TELL HOW LONG HE'D BEEN TRAVELING.

SHUNA KILLED
TO EAT.

SURVIVAL
BECAME A
STRUGGLE.

WAIT, NO: SHUNA COULD HEAR A MUFFLED WEEPING.
THE SOUND OF THE WEEPING DIED AWAY AMONG THE DUNES...

THE ATTACKERS
LEFT AS SILENTLY
AS THEY HAD
COME.

THE FRAGMENTS STREWN ACROSS THE GROUND HAD CLEARLY BEEN HUMAN BONES. THERE WERE SIGNS THAT THEY HAD BEEN BAKED AND SNAPPED OPEN, AND HAD THE MARROW SUCKED OUT.

WALKING TO WHERE THE WOMAN HAD POINTED, SHUNA FOUND AN OPENING THAT LOOKED LIKE AN ENTRANCE.

THERE WAS A DRY CRUNCHING SOUND AS HE WALKED. A COLD SHIVER RAN UP HIS SPINE.

I AM A TRAVELER IN NEED. COULD I TROUBLE YOU FOR A NIGHT'S FOOD AND SHELTER?

THE SHIP WAS VAST—IT HAD PROBABLY NEVER SET SAIL—AND IT WAS STARTING TO FALL INTO RUIN.

ONE MONTH AFTER LEAVING THE VALLEY, SHUNA SAW WISPS OF SMOKE RISING ON THE DISTANT HORIZON.

IT WAS A SHIP BUILT FROM TIMBER AND STONE.

THERE WERE ONLY RELICS PEOPLE HAD LEFT BEHIND, WHICH WERE STARTING TO RECEDE INTO THE MISTS OF TIME.

RUST-STAINED WATER STRETCHED AS FAR AS THE EYE COULD SEE, FILLING THE HOLLOWS WHERE THE LAND HAD ERODED. A STRANGE, UNPLEASANT SMELL DRIFTED ON THE WIND. FOR DAYS ON END, SHUNA AND THE YAKUL PROCEEDED WESTWARD WITHOUT SEEING ANOTHER LIVING THING.

TO THE WEST

UNDER
A NEW MOON,
AS THE PEOPLE
SLEPT, SHUNA
BROKE THE LAW
OF THE KINGDOM
AND SADDLED
HIS YAKUL.

YET THE TIME CAME TO LEAVE; NOBODY COULD HOLD THE YOUNG MAN BACK... THE ELDERS SIGHED SADLY.

THE WOMEN SAW SHUNA PREPARE MORE BULLETS THAN HE WOULD TAKE ON HUNTS, AND THEY REALIZED HIS MIND WAS MADE UP.

HIS FATHER AND THE ELDERS WERE WORRIED AND TRIED TO TALK HIM ROUND. "WE MAY BE POOR," THEY SAID, "BUT SUCH IS OUR FATE, AND IT IS RIGHT THAT WE BE BURIED HERE IN THIS EARTH."

SHUNA SAID, "OUR HIWABIE SEEDS ARE SMALL AND MEAGER. WOULD YOU GIVE US THESE?"

"I COULD, BUT THERE WOULD BE NO USE IN SOWING THEM... THESE SEEDS HAVE HAD THEIR HULLS REMOVED: THEY ARE DEAD. I HAVE HEARD LIVING SEEDS ARE ENCASED IN A GOLDEN HULL THAT SHINES BEAUTIFULLY...

"ALL THESE YEARS, I HAVE TRAVELED IN SEARCH OF THAT GOLDEN GRAIN, HOPING TO RELIEVE MY PEOPLE OF THEIR SUFFERING, BUT NOW I AM OLD... MY STRENGTH IS GONE..."

THE POUCH CONTAINED SEEDS THAT WERE LIKE NOTHING SHUNA HAD EVER SEEN. "THESE WERE GIVEN TO ME BY THAT TRAVELER. THEY SAY THOSE WHO POSSESS THIS GRAIN WILL WANT FOR NOTHING AND NEVER KNOW HUNGER OR STRIFE..." THE SEEDS WERE LARGE AND HEAVY.

THE TRAVELER BECKONED SHUNA TO HIS DEATHBED. "I AM THE PRINCE OF A DISTANT COUNTRY IN THE EAST. IT WAS A POOR COUNTRY, AND HUNGER ALWAYS PLAGUED OUR PEOPLE."

THE WISEST OLD HEALER IN THE VALLEY TRIED TO SAVE THE TRAVELER'S LIFE WITH HER SPELLS AND HERBS, BUT IT WAS TOO LATE.

OUTSIDERS RARELY CAME TO THIS VALLEY. IT WAS THE PEOPLE'S CUSTOM TO RECEIVE ALL VISITORS AS THEIR GUESTS AND TREAT THEM WITH RESPECT.
1983

THE MAN'S CLOTHES WERE UNFAMILIAR: HE WAS NOT FROM AROUND HERE. HUNGER AND EXHAUSTION HAD LEFT HIM AT DEATH'S DOOR.

SAD AND IMPOVERISHED WERE THEIR LIVES.

BEAUTIFUL AND BRUTAL WAS THE NATURE THEY LIVED IN.
THE BOY'S NAME WAS SHUNA. ONE DAY, HE WOULD TAKE OVER FROM HIS FATHER AS RULER OF THE KINGDOM.

EVEN SO, THE PEOPLE
WERE GRATEFUL
FOR THEIR MODEST
HARVESTS...
THEY WORKED
THEMSELVES INTO
THE GROUND,
THEN THEY DIED...

WITH SO LITTLE GRASS TO EAT, THE YAKUL WERE ALWAYS STARVING, AND THEY RARELY BORE YOUNG...

THE PEOPLE SCRAPED THE DRY SOIL AND PLANTED HIWABIE SEEDLINGS, YET THE BARREN LAND YIELDED ONLY THE SLIGHTEST OF CROPS.

WHY DID PEOPLE EVER SETTLE IN A LAND LIKE THIS?
THE WIND BLOWING DOWN FROM THE MOUNTAINS TURNED THE THIN AIR EVEN THINNER, AND THE SUN'S WARMTH NEVER REACHED THE VALLEY.

THESE THINGS MAY HAVE HAPPENED LONG AGO; THEY MAY BE STILL TO COME. NO ONE REALLY KNOWS ANYMORE.
THE JOURNEY BEGINS
AT THE BOTTOM OF AN ANCIENT VALLEY CARVED OUT BY A GLACIER, THERE WAS A SMALL KINGDOM WHICH TIME HAD ABANDONED.

CONTENTS

HAYAO MIYAZAKI

Shuna's Journey

TRANSLATED BY
ALEX DUDOK DE WIT

:01
First Second
NEW YORK

Shuna's Journey